국제학교 학생이 말하는
공립학교 vs 국제학교

국제학교 학생이 말하는
공립학교 VS 국제학교

목차

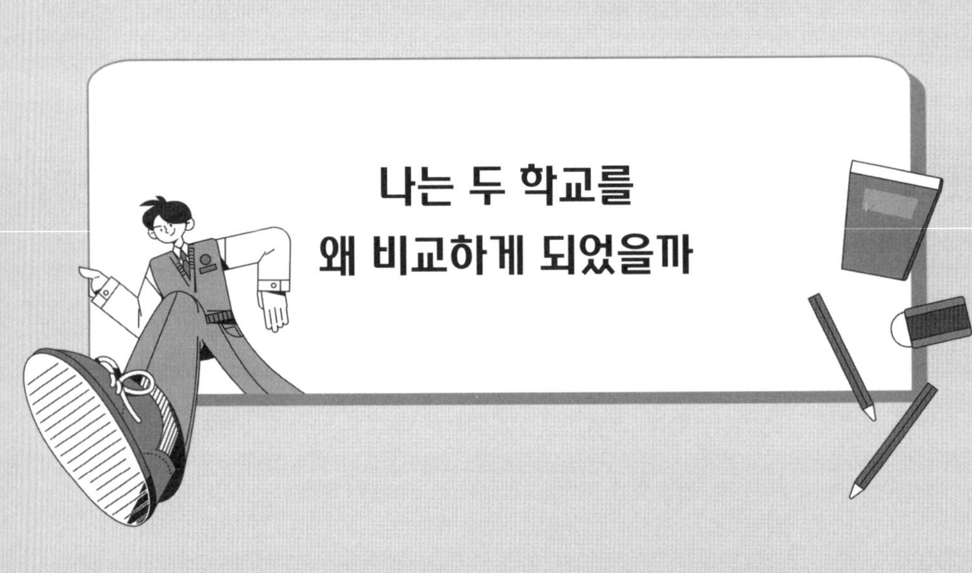

나는 두 학교를
왜 비교하게 되었을까

"나는 두 학교를 왜 비교하게 되었을까?"

내가 처음 공립학교에 입학했을 때, 내 인생은 그럭저럭 했다.

모두가 같은 방향을 바라보며 공부하던 교실,

시험 점수, 반 등수, 교과서 진도,

모든 것이 똑같다고 느껴졌다.

하지만 어느 날, 부모님께서 뜻밖의 제안을 하셨다.

"국제학교에 전학 가보는 건 어때?"

솔직히 말하면 처음엔 당황했다.

'국제학교? 영어로 수업을 해? 외국인 친구들하고 같이 공부해? 나한테 맞을까?'

그때는 국제학교가 뭔지도 몰랐고, '그냥 비싼 학교' 정도로만 생각했다.

그리고 그 선택은 내 인생의 많은 걸 바꿨다.

교실 분위기부터 선생님과의 거리, 친구들의 태도, 평가 방식까지.

이전 공립학교에서 배운 방식과는 너무도 다른 세상이었다.

좋은 점도 있었지만, 당황스러운 점도 있었다.

그제서야 나는 스스로에게 물었다.

'내가 지금까지 다녔던 공립학교와, 지금의 국제학교는 대체 뭐가 그렇게 다른 걸까?'

이 책은 그 질문에서 시작되었다.

단순히 학교를 나열하고 비교하는 책이 아니다.

직접 두 세계를 경험한 학생으로서, 그 안에서 느꼈던 리얼한 **차이점**을 하나하나 풀어보려 한다.

혹시 당신도 두 학교 사이에서 고민하고 있진 않은가?

혹은 자녀에게 어떤 교육 환경이 더 맞을지 고민 중인가?

그렇다면, 지금부터 내 이야기가 조금은 도움이 될 수 있을지도 모른다.

"Why Did I Start Comparing These Two Schools?"

When I first entered a public school, life was··· well, just fine.

A classroom where everyone was facing the same direction,
focused on the same goals—test scores, class rankings, and
textbook progress.
Everything felt identical. Predictable.

But one day, my parents brought up something unexpected:
"How about transferring to an international school?"

To be honest, I was confused.
"An international school? Classes in English? Studying with foreign
kids? Would that even suit me?"
At the time, I didn't know what an international school was.
I just thought of it as "one of those really expensive schools."

That choice ended up changing a lot in my life.
From the classroom atmosphere to how close we were with
teachers,
from how my friends acted to how we were graded—
Everything felt completely different from the public school I used
to know.

Some changes were exciting. Others were confusing.

And for the first time, I asked myself:

"What exactly makes my old public school so different from this international one?"

This book begins with that very question.

It's not just a list of school features or a surface-level comparison.

It's a real story—from a student who experienced both sides.

The things that surprised me, challenged me, and opened my mind.

Maybe you're also stuck between the two.

Or maybe you're a parent wondering what kind of school fits your child best.

If so, then maybe—just maybe—my story might help a little.

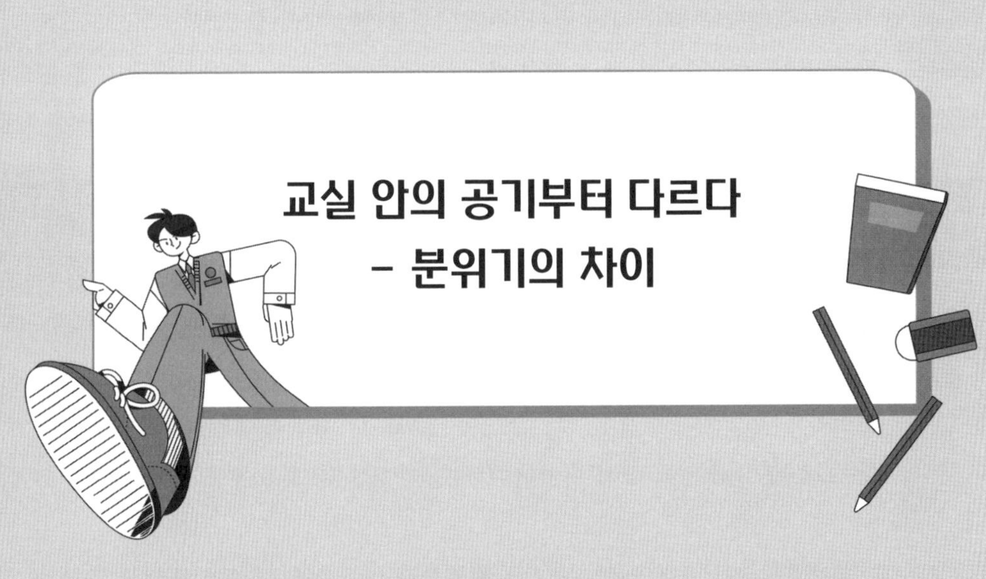

교실 안의 공기부터 다르다
– 분위기의 차이

교실 안의 공기부터 다르다 – 분위기의 차이

처음 국제학교에 전학 가던 날이 아직도 생생하게 기억난다.

가장 먼저 눈에 들어온 건 교실의 분위기였다.

책상 배열부터 달랐고, 학생들은 삼삼오오 모여 이야기하거나 서로의 노트북 화면을 들여다보고 있었다.

딱히 수업이 시작된 것 같진 않았지만, 모두가 뭔가에 몰두해 있는 느낌이었다.

분명 교복을 입고 있었지만, 자세나 표정은 훨씬 자연스럽고 편안해 보였다.

목소리는 자유롭게 오갔고, 때로는 웃음소리도 스치듯 들려왔다.

말 그대로 '살아 있는 교실'이었다.

그에 비해, 내가 다녔던 공립학교는 훨씬 정돈되고 조용한 공간이었다.

교실에 들어서면 대부분의 학생들이 말없이 자리에 앉아 있었고,

수업 전에는 개인 공부를 하거나 책을 읽는 분위기가 익숙했다.

목소리를 높이거나 자리를 벗어나는 건 조금 눈치가 보였고,

수업 시간엔 선생님의 설명을 조용히 받아 적는 것이 기본이었다.

모두가 성실했고 열심이었지만, 그 열심은 어딘가 긴장된 공기 속에 간

혀 있었다.

　국제학교는 달랐다.

　질문은 자유롭게 튀어나왔고, 친구들끼리 아이디어를 주고받으며 배우는 느낌이 강했다.

　'조용한 교실'이 아니라, 생각이 활발히 오가는 공간이었다.

　그 다름은 단순히 시스템의 차이가 아니라, 수업을 대하는 방식 자체의 차이였다.

　국제학교 교실의 그 자유로운 분위기는 나에게 신선한 충격이었다.

　하지만 동시에, 어디선가 '이렇게 자유로워도 괜찮은 걸까?' 하는 불안감도 밀려왔다.

　질문하고 발표하는 것이 자연스러워 보였지만, 내가 잘못 말하면 어떻게 될지 몰라 긴장되었다.

　처음 며칠은 그 긴장감 때문에 오히려 말수를 줄이고, 조용히 상황을 지켜보는 데 급급했다.

　그러나 시간이 지날수록 조금씩 분위기에 익숙해졌다.

　친구들이 틀려도 서로 웃어 넘기고, 다시 의견을 내는 모습을 보며 마음이 놓였다.

　선생님들도 실수를 크게 문제 삼지 않고, 오히려 더 많은 질문을 권장하는 듯했다.

　나도 점점 자유롭게 내 생각을 표현하는 법을 배우기 시작했다.

　그 자유 속에서, '틀림'에 대한 두려움이 조금씩 사라졌고,

대신 '도전'과 '호기심'이 교실 안을 가득 채우는 것을 느꼈다.

이렇게 적응하면서 나는 배움이란 단순히 '정답'을 맞히는 것이 아니라, 서로 다른 생각들이 부딪히고 섞여 새로워지는 과정임을 깨닫게 되었다.
그 변화는 내게 학업뿐 아니라 인생에 있어서도 중요한 깨달음이 되었다.

The Air Inside the Classroom Felt Different
– A Shift in Atmosphere

I still vividly remember my first day at the international school.

What struck me the most was the atmosphere in the classroom.

The desks were arranged differently.

Students were chatting in small groups or looking at each other's laptop screens.

The class hadn't even started yet, but everyone seemed deeply focused on something.

They were in uniform, sure—but their postures and expressions looked much more relaxed and natural.

Voices flowed freely through the room, and now and then, I caught the sound of light laughter.

In contrast, my old public school classroom had been a much quieter, more controlled space.

It was what you might call a "disciplined" environment.

Most students would sit in silence before class, reading or reviewing notes.

Raising your voice or moving from your seat felt like breaking an unspoken rule.

During lessons, we listened quietly to the teacher and copied notes.

Everyone was diligent and hardworking, but that effort was wrapped in a kind of tense air,

As if we were always preparing for something we couldn't afford to mess up.

The international school was different.

Questions popped up freely.

Students exchanged ideas in real time, often learning just as much from each other as from the teacher.

It wasn't a "quiet classroom" anymore—it was a space full of active, buzzing thoughts.

And that difference wasn't just about classroom layout or school rules;

It reflected a completely different attitude toward learning.

That freedom in the classroom was a culture shock at first.

Part of me wondered: "Is it okay to be this relaxed?"

As much as it looked natural for others to ask questions or speak up,

I was nervous—what if I said something wrong?

During those first few days, I mostly kept quiet,

Carefully observing the flow of things rather than joining in.

But as time went on, something changed.

I saw how mistakes were met with laughter, not embarrassment.

Friends would try again without hesitation, and teachers didn't treat errors like failures.

They encouraged more questions, more ideas.

Slowly, I began to speak up, too.

The fear of being wrong started to fade.

In its place came curiosity—and the confidence to explore it.

Through that process, I realized learning wasn't just about getting the right answer.

It was about clashing, sharing, and mixing different perspectives until something new emerged.

That shift didn't just change how I studied.

It changed how I thought—and that made all the difference.

수업 방식의 차이
– 자유와 체계 사이

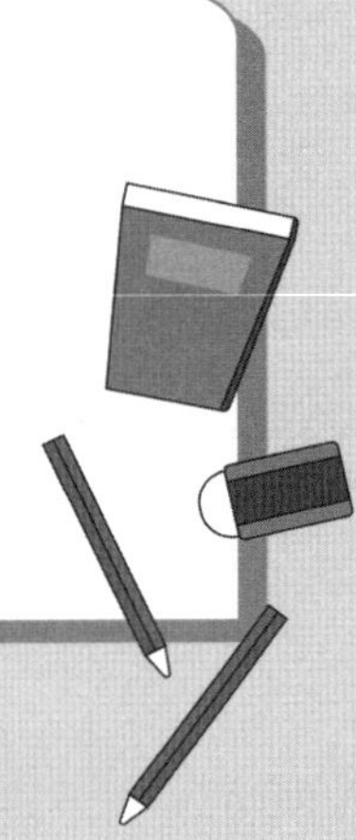

수업 방식의 차이 – 자유와 체계 사이

국제학교 수업은 늘 활기차고 역동적이었다.

선생님은 학생들에게 질문을 던지고, 학생들은 자신의 생각을 거리낌 없이 표현했다.

작은 토론이 자연스럽게 이어졌고, 친구들과 의견을 주고받는 과정에서 배우는 재미가 컸다.

틀린 답도 자유롭게 말할 수 있었고, 그것조차 배움의 일부였다.

내가 처음 국제학교에서 제일 놀랐던 건 '교과서가 없다는 것'이었다.

정확히 말하면, 모든 과목에 딱 정해진 책 한 권이 있는 게 아니었다. 수업에 따라 온라인 자료, 영상, 뉴스 기사, 심지어 TED 강연이나 유튜브 콘텐츠까지 활용됐다.

'수업=교과서'라고 생각했던 나에겐 꽤 충격이었다.

처음엔 좀 어지럽고 갈피를 잡기 어려웠지만, 어느 순간 다양한 자료들을 넘나들며 배우는 게 훨씬 생생하게 느껴졌다.

내가 다녔던 공립학교는 분위기가 조금 달랐다.

수업은 정해진 교과서를 중심으로 차근차근 진행됐고, 선생님은 내용 전달에 집중했다.

학생들은 조용히 필기를 하거나 발표 내용을 듣는 데 익숙했고, 질문은 손을 들어 타이밍을 맞춰야 했지만, 그만큼 수업 흐름이 또렷하고 안정감이 있었다.

모두가 나름의 집중 방식으로 공부했고, 서로 방해되지 않도록 배려하는 문화가 자연스러웠다.

규칙은 분명 존재했지만, 그 안에서 나름의 질서와 효율이 있었던 것이다.

그렇다고 국제학교가 항상 편하기만 했던 건 아니다.

자기 주도적으로 움직여야 했기 때문에, '가만히 있어도 알아서 흘러가는 수업'은 없었다.

준비를 안 해 오면 바로 드러났고, 토론이나 발표에서는 자신의 생각을 말로 정리하는 능력이 필수였다.

누군가의 생각을 듣고 반응하는 것도 하나의 숙제였고, 가끔은 머릿속이 뒤죽박죽이 되기도 했다.

반면, 공립학교에서는 일단 정해진 흐름 안에 있으니 덜 헤맸다.

공부의 방향이 명확했고, 필요한 내용을 차근차근 쌓아가는 느낌이었다.

모르는 게 있으면 참고서나 문제집을 펼치면 됐고, 선생님이 정리해주는 개념을 그대로 따라가면 큰 혼란은 없었다.

그 점이 오히려 지금 와서 보면 꽤 큰 장점이기도 했다.

돌이켜보면, 두 환경은 각각 다른 방식으로 나를 훈련시켰다.

하나는 내 안에 있는 질문을 꺼내게 만들었고,

다른 하나는 깊이 있게 파고드는 습관을 들이게 했다.

그리고 그 둘이 합쳐지면서, 나는 더 균형 있게 '생각하고 배우는 법'을 **익혀 나가게** 된 것 같다.

처음엔 국제학교 방식이 너무 자유로워 혼란스러웠지만, 점차 그 속에서 내 생각을 키울 수 있었다.

공립학교의 차분한 구조와 국제학교의 유연한 흐름은 너무 달랐지만,

두 방식 모두 '공부'라는 같은 목표를 향해 다른 길을 걷는 느낌이었다.

Different Ways of Learning
– Between Freedom and Structure

Classes at the international school were always lively and dynamic.

Teachers asked questions constantly, and students shared their thoughts without hesitation.

Discussions often happened spontaneously, and learning through exchanging ideas with classmates

made the experience all the more engaging.

Even wrong answers were welcome—it was all part of the learning process.

What surprised me most when I first came to the international school was this:

There were no official textbooks.

To be more accurate, there wasn't a single, fixed book for every subject.

Depending on the class, we used online articles, videos, news reports, even TED Talks or YouTube clips.

For someone like me, who had always equated "class" with "textbook," it was a real shock.

At first, it felt a little chaotic and hard to follow.

But over time, I realized that learning through such a variety of sources made things feel more vivid and real.

Things had been quite different at the public school I attended before.

Lessons followed a set textbook, step by step, and teachers focused on delivering content.

Students were used to listening quietly or taking notes.

Questions were asked only after raising your hand at the right moment.

The structure brought clarity and stability to the flow of the class.

Everyone had their way of focusing, and there was an unspoken culture of not disturbing one another.

Rules were definitely present, but there was a sense of order and efficiency within them.

That doesn't mean international school was always easy or comfortable.

You had to take initiative—there were no classes where you could just sit back and let the lesson carry you.

If you came unprepared, it showed immediately.

In discussions or presentations, you had to clearly articulate your thoughts, and listening to others and responding thoughtfully was just as important.

Sometimes, it felt like my mind was spinning in a hundred

directions.

At the public school, on the other hand, I rarely felt that lost.

There was a clear direction to the studying, and it felt like we were steadily building up the knowledge we needed.

If you didn't understand something, you could turn to a workbook or a guidebook.

As long as you followed the teacher's explanations, things stayed relatively straightforward.

Looking back, that clarity was a big strength.

In the end, both learning environments trained me in different but equally valuable ways.

One encouraged me to voice the questions inside me.

The other taught me how to dig deep and stay focused.

Together, they helped me learn how to think and study in a more balanced way.

At first, I was overwhelmed by how unstructured the international school seemed.

But as time went on, I realized it gave me space to develop my thinking.

The quiet structure of a public school and the flexible rhythm of an international school were completely different—

But both were heading toward the same goal: learning.

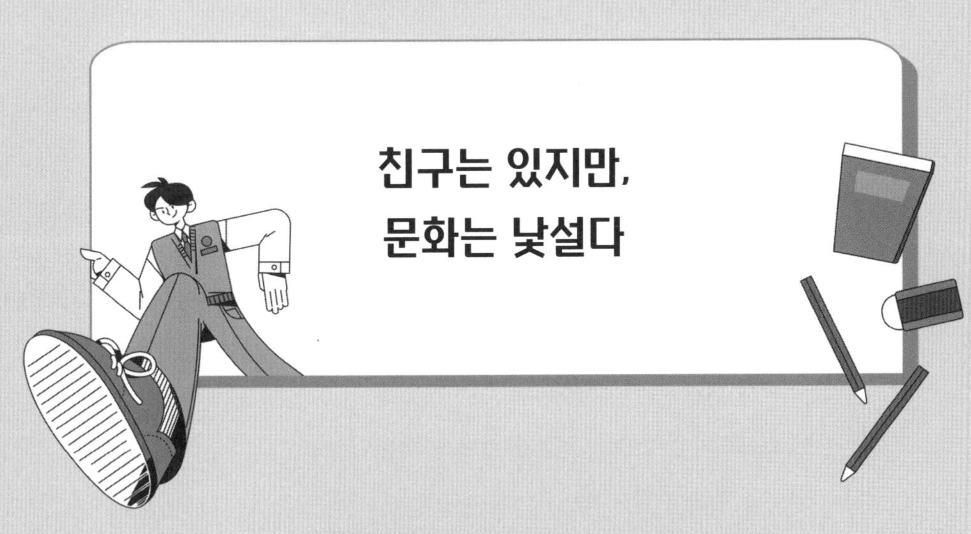

친구는 있지만, 문화는 낯설다

친구는 있지만, 문화는 낯설다

국제학교에 전학 간 지 며칠 되지 않았을 때,

나에게 먼저 **다가와** 준 친구들이 있었다.

"Where are you from?", "Do you play any sports?" 같은 가벼운

질문으로 말을 걸어줬고,

점심시간에도 같이 앉자고 손짓해 줬다.

분명 따뜻하고 배려 있는 모습이었지만,

그 속에서 나는 왠지 조금 다른 세계에 발을 디딘 느낌이었다.

다들 영어를 너무 자연스럽게, 너무 빠르게 썼다.

유머도, 눈치도, 말장난도 전부 영어로 이뤄졌다.

나는 문장은 알아들었지만,

그 분위기와 속도에 맞춰 반응하는 건 또 다른 문제였다.

웃어야 할 타이밍을 놓치거나,

질문을 받았는데 대답을 머뭇거리게 되는 일이 자주 있었다.

그때마다 괜히 내 어깨가 움츠러들었다.

공립학교에서는 친구들과 다 똑같은 교복을 입고,

똑같은 급식을 먹고, 비슷한 말투로 이야기했다.
말이 통하는 친구들 사이에 있었기에,
친해지는 데 많은 에너지가 필요하지 않았다.
서로 눈치껏 다가가고, 익숙한 분위기 속에서 자연스럽게 친해졌다.
하지만 국제학교에서는 문화 자체가 너무 다르기 때문에
말이 통해도 '진짜 친해지는 데'는 시간이 더 오래 걸렸다.

어떤 날은
내가 그냥 조용히 있는 걸 '낯가리는 것'이 아니라
'비사교적'으로 보는 건 아닐까 걱정도 됐다.
"너는 왜 항상 말이 없어?" 같은 말에 당황하기도 했다.
하지만 시간이 지나면서 알게 됐다.
그들은 단지 나와 다른 방식으로 소통하고, 다른 방식으로 친해지는 것
뿐이었다는 걸.

Friends, But Still Foreign
— When Culture Feels Distant

Just a few days after I transferred to the international school,

Some classmates came up to me and started conversations.

"Where are you from?" "Do you play any sports?"

They smiled, gestured for me to sit with them at lunch, and welcomed me warmly.

It was kind and considerate—but somehow, I still felt like I had stepped into a different world.

Everyone spoke English so naturally, so quickly.

Jokes, inside references, even subtle cues—they all happened in English.

I could understand the words,

but reacting at the right time, with the right tone, was a whole other challenge.

Sometimes I missed the moment to laugh,

or hesitated when someone asked me a question.

Each time that happened, I felt myself shrink a little inside.

At my old public school, we all wore the same uniform,

ate the same lunch, and spoke in the same way.

Because I was surrounded by people who shared my language and habits,

Making friends didn't take much effort.

We understood each other quickly, without having to explain much.

But at the international school, the culture itself was so different

That even though we spoke the same language,

It took longer to truly connect.

Some days, I worried that being quiet might come across the wrong way.

What if they didn't see me as shy,

But as unfriendly or uninterested?

I remember feeling confused when someone said,

"Why are you always so quiet?"

But over time, I began to understand—

They weren't trying to judge me.

They just communicated differently.

They had their ways of showing interest, of becoming close.

And slowly, I started to learn those ways too.

같은 나이, 다른 세계

같은 나이, 다른 세계

● ● ● ● ●

국제학교에 처음 들어갔을 때
가장 낯설었던 건 사실 친구들이었어.

겉보기엔 다 비슷했지.
나처럼 11살이고, 교복을 입고, 점심시간엔 농담도 하고.
그런데 조금만 깊게 얘기해 보면,
각자가 살아온 배경과 생각이 너무나 달랐어.

내 옆자리에 앉은 친구는 어릴 때 프랑스에서 살다 왔고,
또 어떤 친구는 매일 집에서 3개국어를 쓰며 자랐다고 했지.

처음엔 솔직히 주눅이 들기도 했어.
'나는 영어도 한국어도 완벽하진 않은데…'
'나는 어디 특별한 데 다녀본 적도 없는데…'
나도 모르게 스스로를 작게 만들고 있었던 거야.

"너희 나라에선 어때?"

Global Perspectives 수업에서
난민 문제를 다룰 때였어.
다들 국가별 입장에서 토론을 하는 수업이었는데,
한 친구가 내게 물었어.

"Siwoo, 한국에선 난민에 대해 어떻게 생각해?"

나는 머뭇거리다가
"사실 깊게 생각해본 적 없는데…"라고 대답했지.
그랬더니 그 친구는
"그래? 그럼, 이번에 같이 조사해 볼래?"라며 나를 팀에 끼워줬어.

같이 조사를 하다 보니,
그 친구는 아랍계 난민 가족 출신이었고,
그래서 난민 문제를 굉장히 현실적으로 느끼고 있었더라고.
나는 말했어.

"나는 그냥 뉴스에서만 봤어.
이렇게 가까이에서 얘기해 본 건 처음이야."

그 친구는 웃으면서

"이제부터 같이 생각해 보면 되지!"라고 말했어.

그 순간 알았어.
서로 다른 건 이상한 게 아니라,
같이 이야기할 수 있는 기회라는 걸.

친구가 나를 넓혀준다
국제학교 친구들과 얘기하면서 느낀 건,
내가 모르는 게 너무 많다는 사실이었어.

하지만 그걸 부끄러워하지 않아도 된다는 것도 배웠지.
왜냐면 여긴,

"너 그거 몰라?"가 아니라
"같이 알아보자."라고 말해주는 공간이었으니까.

- 어떤 친구는 일본 애니메이션과 한국 웹툰의 차이를 진지하게 분석하고,
- 또 다른 친구는 축구보다 넷볼이 더 재미있다며 열정적으로 설명했어.
- 누군가는 매일 명상 수업 끝나고 '오늘의 감정'을 공유했지.

이런 친구들을 보면서
나도 나만의 시선과 이야기를 갖고 싶은 마음이 생겼어.

그리고 어느 날, 나도 누군가에게 물었어.

"너는 어떻게 생각해?"

내가 넓어지는 순간
이제는 알아.
진짜 친구는 나를 편하게 해주는 사람만이 아니라,
나를 더 넓게 만들어주는 사람이라는 걸.

국제학교에 와서 내가 만난 친구들은
나를 비판하지 않았고,
내 말을 기다려줬고,
내가 모르는 세상을 보여줬어.

그리고 나도 그들에게
내 이야기를 꺼내는 법을 배웠어.

Same Age, Different Worlds

When I first entered the international school,
What felt most unfamiliar wasn't the language or the classes.
It was the **people**—the friends.

On the surface, we all seemed the same.
Fifteen years old, wearing school uniforms,
Laughing over jokes during lunch.
But the moment I got to know them a little deeper,
I realized that each of them had such a different story,
A different world behind their smile.

The classmate next to me had lived in France as a child.
Another spoke three languages at home every day.

At first, I felt small.
"I'm not fluent in English or even Korean⋯"
"I've never lived anywhere special⋯"
Without realizing it, I was shrinking myself—
Thinking I didn't belong.

"What's it like in your country?"

It happened during a Global Perspectives class,

When we were discussing the refugee crisis.

We were asked to debate from different national viewpoints,

And one student turned to me and asked,

"Siwoo, what do people in Korea think about refugees?"

I hesitated.

"Honestly⋯ I've never really thought about it."

They smiled and said,

"No problem. Want to research it together?"

As we worked on the topic, I learned that this student's family had once been refugees.

For them, the issue wasn't just academic—it was personal.

I told them,

"I've only ever seen this on the news.

I've never talked about it with someone who's lived it."

They replied,

"Well, now you have. Let's keep thinking about it together."

And in that moment, I realized something—

Being different wasn't strange.

It was an **invitation to connect.**

Friends Who Expand You

Talking with my classmates at the international school,

I started to realize just how much I didn't know.

But more importantly, I learned that I didn't need to be ashamed of that.

Because here,

No one said, "You don't know that?"

Instead, they said,

"Let's find out together."

One friend would dive deep into the differences between Japanese anime and Korean webtoons.

Another passionately explained why they loved netball more than soccer.

Some students would share their emotions after a daily meditation session.

And slowly, I started to want that too—

A perspective that was **uniquely mine.**

Something I could share with others.

And one day, I found myself asking someone,

"What do you think about this?"

The Moment I Grew

Now I know—

A true friend isn't just someone who makes you feel comfortable.

It's someone **who expands your world.**

The friends I met at the international school didn't judge me.

They waited for me to speak.

They showed me parts of the world I'd never seen.

And in return,

They taught me how to share my story, too.

선생님과의 관계

선생님과의 관계

혹시 너도 그랬어?

공립학교에선 '선생님' 하면 뭔가 자동으로 긴장이 되잖아.

말할 때도 존댓말, 질문할 때도 "죄송한데요…"로 시작해야 할 것 같고.

수업 중에 농담이라도 치면 눈총 받기 일쑤고,

방과 후에 선생님을 따로 만나는 건 거의 불가능했지.

그런데 국제학교에선 그 분위기가 완전히 달랐어.

첫날 수업이 끝나고 나서였어.

내가 좀 헷갈리는 게 있어서 자리에서 머뭇거리는데,

선생님이 먼저 다가오더니 이렇게 말했어.

"Hey, do you want to talk through that part again together?"

'Talk together?'

그 말이 이상하게 마음에 남았어.

내가 틀렸다는 게 아니라, 같이 다시 생각해 보자는 느낌.

그게 그냥 말투만 그런 게 아니었어.
질문을 하면 선생님은 답을 바로 주기보단,
"그건 네가 어떻게 생각해?" 하고 되물으셨어.
이게 처음엔 살짝 부담스럽기도 했지만,
나중엔 진짜 '생각하는 법'을 배우게 됐어.

그리고 이건 내가 진짜 놀랐던 순간인데,
어느 날 점심시간에 선생님이 학생 몇 명이랑
같은 테이블에 앉아서 햄버거를 먹고 있었어.
그냥 학생처럼 웃고 떠들면서.
물론 서로를 존중하는 선은 있었지만,
그 안엔 위아래가 아닌 수평적인 신뢰감이 있었어.

국제학교에서 선생님은
지식을 전달하는 사람이라기보단
함께 배우는 가이드 같았어.
내가 어떤 주제를 더 깊게 파고들고자 하면,
그걸 전적으로 응원해줬고,
때로는 수업 시간을 넘어서까지 자료를 같이 찾아주기도 했어.

그래서 그런지, 국제학교에선 선생님과 '좋은 사이'가 되는 게
그저 친해진다는 의미가 아니라,
서로에 대한 신뢰가 쌓인다는 느낌이 강했어.

정답을 가르쳐주는 대신,
"넌 어떤 방향으로 생각하고 싶어?"라고 묻는 선생님.
그런 어른을 만난다는 게 얼마나 큰 행운인지,
나는 그때는 몰랐지만 지금은 확실히 알아.

Teachers: From Authority to Ally

Did you ever feel that way, too?

Back in my public school, the word "teacher" almost automatically made me tense.

You had to speak in honorifics,

And even when asking a question, you'd start with something like,

"Excuse me, I'm sorry to bother you, but…"

Making a joke in class? That was risky.

And seeing a teacher outside class hours? Nearly impossible.

But in the international school,

Everything felt completely different.

After my very first class,

I was lingering at my desk, confused about something.

Then the teacher walked over and said,

"Hey, do you want to talk through that part again together?"

"Talk together"?

That phrase stuck with me.

It didn't sound like I had gotten something wrong.

It sounded like we'd figure it out together.

And it wasn't just a nice way of speaking.

When I asked a question, instead of giving me the answer,

The teacher would say,
"What do you think?"

At first, that actually made me a bit uncomfortable.
But over time, I started learning how to really **think for myself.**

Lunch with the Teacher

One moment still feels surreal.
One lunchtime, I saw a teacher sitting with a few students,
eating hamburgers and laughing with them like it was the most natural thing in the world
Sure, there was still respect—
But it wasn't about power or authority.
It felt like trust, built sideways, not top-down.

At the international school,
Teachers weren't just knowledge-givers.
They were like **guides,** walking with us.

If I wanted to dive deeper into a topic,
They would cheer me on.
Sometimes they even helped me find extra resources outside class.
It didn't just feel like "getting along with the teacher."

It felt like being in a relationship built on mutual curiosity and trust.

A teacher who doesn't hand you the answer,
but instead asks,
"Which direction do you want to explore?"
Back then, I didn't fully realize what a gift that was.
Now, I do.

선생님과의 관계
: 배움의 동반자

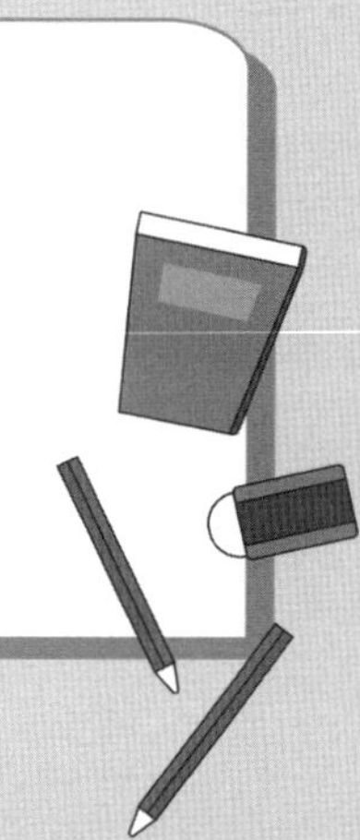

선생님과의 관계: 배움의 동반자

● ● ● ● ●

국제학교에 다니면서 가장 놀라웠던 것 중 하나는, 선생님과 학생 사이의 '거리'였어.

그 거리가 멀다는 뜻이 아니라, 너무 가깝고 자연스럽다는 의미로.

수업이 끝나면 학생들이 먼저 선생님 책상으로 다가가서 질문을 던지고, 어떤 날은 그냥 "주말 잘 보내셨어요?" 같은 인사로 대화를 시작하기도 해.

심지어 점심시간이나 쉬는 시간에 선생님과 나란히 앉아서 이야기하는 모습도 흔했어.

이전 학교에선 상상도 못 했던 장면이었지.

수업 중에도 마찬가지야.

"이건 왜 그래요?", "제 생각은 이건데요…"

이런 질문과 의견이 오가는 게 전혀 눈치 보이지 않고,

선생님도 진심으로 반응해 줘.

질문이 틀렸다고 혼내는 일도 없고,

오히려 "좋은 질문이야."라며 칭찬해 주는 경우가 많아.

이런 분위기 덕분에 선생님을 점점 두려운 존재가 아니라,
함께 배우고 성장하는 배움의 파트너처럼 느끼게 됐어.
물론 숙제나 평가에서는 엄격한 부분도 있지만,
그 과정에서도 선생님은 늘 피드백을 주고,
내가 뭘 더 잘할 수 있을지를 같이 고민해 줘.

가끔은 수업과 관련 없는 인생 이야기, 진로 고민,
심지어 친구 관계까지도 편하게 상담할 수 있었어.
그런 게 쌓이다 보니,
"이 선생님은 나를 그냥 한 명의 학생이 아니라
한 사람으로 진심을 다해 봐주고 있구나."라는 생각이 들었지.

이전 학교에선 선생님이 높은 곳에 있는 존재처럼 느껴졌다면,
여기선 정말 같은 눈높이에서 걷고 있는 어른이라는 느낌이었어.
그리고 그게 내가 배움에 더 열정을 갖게 된 이유 중 하나였던 것 같아.

A Partner in Learning
: Rethinking the Teacher–Student Relationship

One of the things that surprised me the most at my international school

was the distance—or lack of it—between students and teachers.

And by **"distance," I don't mean we were far apart.**

Quite the opposite—everything felt closer, more natural.

After class, students would casually walk up to the teacher's desk

with questions.

Sometimes they'd just start a chat with,

"How was your weekend?"

It wasn't strange at all to see students and teachers

sitting side by side at lunch or during breaks.

Back in my old school, that would've been unimaginable.

It was the same during class.

"Why is it like that?"

"Here's what I think⋯"

Questions and opinions flowed freely, without anyone feeling

self-conscious.

And teachers didn't just tolerate it—they welcomed it.

Even if your question wasn't perfectly worded,

They often responded with,

"That's a great question."

This kind of atmosphere gradually changed how I saw my teachers.
They didn't feel like distant authority figures anymore.
They became **partners in learning**—people I could grow alongside.

Sure, there were still rules, assignments, and grades.
But even then, teachers offered thoughtful feedback,
And they genuinely helped me figure out how to do better.
Sometimes we'd even talk about things far beyond the syllabus—
career questions, personal worries,
or challenges with friends.

As those conversations built up over time,
I realized something important:
"This teacher doesn't just see me as a student.
They see me as a whole person."

In my previous school, teachers often felt like they were standing way above us.
But here, it felt like they were walking **with** us, side by side.
And I think that's one of the biggest reasons
Why I started to feel truly passionate about learning.

공부는 '이렇게' 하는 거였어

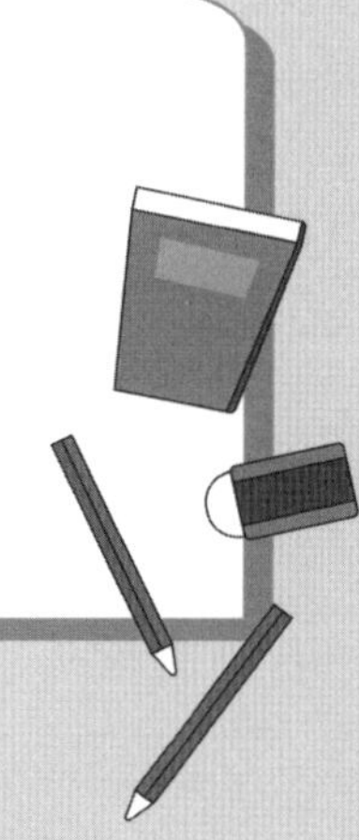

공부는 '이렇게' 하는 거였어?

공립학교에서의 공부는 정해진 틀이 있었어.
공책을 펴고, 선생님이 칠판에 쓰는 걸 따라 적고,
다 외우고, 시험 보고, 끝.

공부가 마치 '게임'처럼 룰이 정해진 것 같았어.
틀린 건 안 되고, 맞아야만 했고,
누가 더 많이 외우느냐가 성적을 결정했지.

그런데 국제학교에 와서는
그 모든 게 완전히 달라졌어.

수업에서 가장 많이 들은 말 중 하나가
"Why?" 그리고 "How do you know?"
답을 맞추는 것보다
그 답에 어떻게 도달했는지가 더 중요했거든.

에세이를 쓸 때도 그냥 정답을 쓰는 게 아니라

내 생각 + 이유 + 근거 자료를 함께 제시해야 했어.
처음엔 너무 어려웠지.
"왜 이렇게 복잡하게 써야 해?" 했는데,
지금 생각해보면 그게 진짜 생각하는 연습이었던 거야.

또, 혼자 하는 공부보다
같이 하는 공부가 많았어.

심지어 시험도 방식이 달라.
객관식도 있긴 하지만,
주관식, 에세이, 발표, 실습 같은 게 훨씬 많아.
시험에서 **틀릴까 봐 불안한 기분**보다,
'**내가 뭘 표현할 수 있을까?**'에 집중하게 되더라.

그리고 정말 놀라운 건,
선생님이 항상 "이건 너의 생각이야?"라고 물어봐 줬다는 거야.
누군가의 정답을 따라가는 게 아니라,
나만의 언어와 방식으로 공부를 해도 괜찮다는 느낌.
이건 공립학교에선 정말 느껴보지 못했던 거였어.

공부가 단순히 성적을 위한 수단이 아니라,
세상을 바라보는 눈을 기르는 도구가 된다는 걸
국제학교에 와서 처음 알았지.

This Is How Studying Was Meant to Be

At my old public school, studying had a fixed routine.
You'd open your notebook, copy what the teacher wrote on the
board,
memorize everything, take the test, and that was it.
Studying felt like a game with strict rules—
no mistakes allowed, only correct answers counted,
And whoever memorized the most got the best grades.

But everything changed when I started at an international school.
One phrase I heard a lot in class was,
"Why?" and "How do you know?"
It wasn't about getting the right answer,
But about how you arrived at that answer.

When writing essays, I couldn't just write the correct facts.
I had to include my thoughts, reasons, and supporting evidence.
At first, it was really hard.
I wondered, "Why does it have to be so complicated?"
But now I realize that was the real practice of thinking.

Also, there was a lot more group work.

Even the exams were different.

There were multiple-choice questions, but more often,

We had essays, presentations, and hands-on tasks.

During tests, I focused less on "What if I get this wrong?"

and more on "How can I express my ideas?"

What surprised me most was that teachers would always ask,

"Is this your thinking?"

It wasn't about following someone else's answer,

But about learning in my way, with my voice.

That's something I never experienced at my old school.

Studying became not just a way to get good grades,

But a tool to develop how I see the world.

That's something I only realized after coming to the international school.

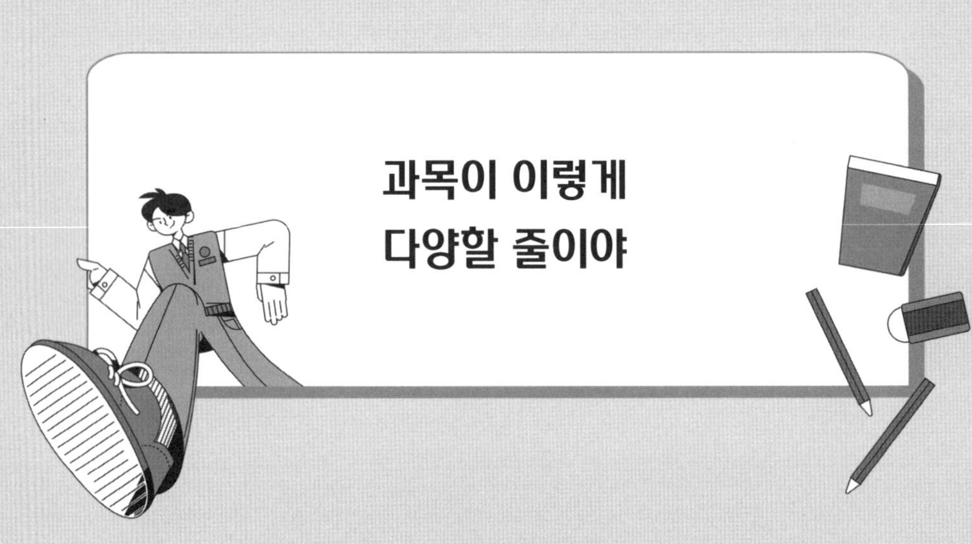
과목이 이렇게
다양할 줄이야

과목이 이렇게 다양할 줄이야

국제학교에 와서 가장 놀란 것 중 하나는,
우리가 배우는 과목 자체였어.

공립학교에선 국어, 수학, 과학, 영어 같은
'딱 정해진 과목'만 있었잖아?
근데 국제학교에서는
INS, UOI, Drama, Media Studies, 같은
처음 들어보는 과목들이 수업 시간표에 당당히 들어 있었어.

처음엔 '이게 진짜 수업이라고?' 싶었지.
하지만 들어가 보니 생각이 **완전히** 바뀌었어.

예를 들어, UOI(Unit of Inquiry) 수업은
하나의 큰 주제를 중심으로
과학, 사회, 언어 같은 다양한 과목 내용을 엮어서 배우는 거야.
예전에 '지속 가능성'을 주제로 배웠던 적이 있었는데,
환경 보호에 대한 자료를 읽고,

플라스틱 사용을 줄이는 방법에 대해 조사하고,
직접 캠페인을 기획하기도 했어.

INS 수업은 역사, 지리, 경제 같은 걸 하나로 엮어서
'세상을 어떻게 바라볼지'를 배우는 과목이었어.
무언가를 외우는 대신, 질문을 던지고, 자료를 분석하고,
내 의견을 글로 정리하는 연습을 계속했지.
가끔은 '이건 진짜 나중에 써먹을 수 있겠다.' 싶은
실전형 과제들도 많았고.

Drama 수업은 말 그대로 신세계였어.
연기 연습을 하면서 감정을 표현하고,
대사 하나를 놓고도 '왜 이 말이 나왔을까?'를 분석했거든.
누가 봐도 '과목'이라기보다 클럽 활동 같았지만,
그 수업을 대하는 태도는 정말 진지했어.

이런 수업들을 하다 보니
자연스럽게 친구들이랑 얘기할 기회도 많아졌고,
서로의 생각을 듣고, 내 생각을 말하는 게 조금씩 편해졌어.

내가 뭘 틀렸는지를 따지는 수업이 아니라,
내가 어떻게 자라고 있는지를 묻는 수업이었다는 점이 정말 달랐어.
단순히 정답과 오답으로 내 머릿속을 평가하지 않았고,
내가 문제를 대하는 태도와 그 과정에서 배우고 깨닫는 점들을 더 중요

하게 여겼지.

처음에는 틀리는 게 두려웠지만,

수업을 거듭할수록 틀림이 '실패'가 아니라 '성장'의 일부라는 걸 깨닫
게 됐어.

그 과정에서 내가 무엇을 배우고, 어떻게 생각이 변하고 있는지,

어떤 새로운 시도를 했는지가 더 소중한 평가 기준이 되었지.

선생님들은 단순한 채점자가 아니라,

내가 더 나은 방향으로 나아가도록 도와주는 가이드 같은 존재였고,

피드백도 항상 "이 부분은 잘했지만, 여기선 이렇게 생각해 보면 더 좋
을 거야."라는 식으로

나의 발전 가능성을 열어 주었어.

그래서 공부는 더 이상 점수 맞추기가 아니라,

내가 조금씩 더 넓은 세상과 깊은 생각을 만나고,

나만의 목소리를 찾아가는 과정이 되었어.

그게 바로 국제학교에서 내가 경험한

'진짜 공부'의 의미였고,

지금도 내 삶과 생각을 움직이게 하는 원동력이 되고 있어.

I Didn't Expect Subjects to Be This Diverse

One of the biggest surprises when I came to the international school was the subjects we studied.

At my old public school, we only had the usual set of subjects —

Korean, math, science, English — the "fixed" ones everyone knows.

But at the international school, the timetable proudly included subjects I'd never even heard of before:

INS, Global Perspectives, Drama, Media Studies.

At first, I thought, "Is this a class?"

But once I stepped inside, my whole perspective changed.

For example, one of the subjects was **UOI (Unit of Inquiry).**

In this class, we explored a big theme by connecting different subjects like science, social studies, and language.

For example, when we learned about sustainability, we read articles about environmental issues, researched ways to reduce plastic use, and even planned our own awareness campaigns.

The goal wasn't just to learn facts —

it was to ask, **"So what can I do with what I've learned?"**

That's when I realized that learning isn't just about knowing things —

it's about figuring out what kind of action I can take in the real world.

INS combined history, geography, and economics into one subject,
Teaching us how to look at the world as a whole.
Instead of memorizing, we asked questions, analyzed data,
And practiced organizing our opinions in writing.
Sometimes the assignments felt very practical —
Like things you could use in real life later on.

Drama class was a whole new world.
We practiced acting to express emotions,
And even took apart a single line to figure out "Why was this said here?"
It looked more like a club activity than a class,
But everyone took it seriously.

Taking these classes naturally gave me more chances to talk with friends,
Listen to their thoughts, and get more comfortable sharing my own.

What stood out was that these classes didn't focus on what I got wrong —

They asked how I was growing.

Instead of grading me by right or wrong answers,

They cared about how I approached problems and what I learned
in the process.

At first, I was afraid of making mistakes,

But as classes went on, I realized mistakes weren't failures —

They were part of the growth.

What mattered more was what I learned, how my thinking
changed,

And what new attempts I made.

Teachers weren't just graders;

They were guides helping me move forward,

Always giving feedback like, "You did well here, but try thinking
this way next time,"

Opening doors for me to improve.

So studying stopped being about chasing grades,

and became a process of meeting a wider world, deeper thoughts,

And finding my voice.

That was the true meaning of "real studying" I experienced at the
international school,

And it's still what drives my life and thinking today.

교실 밖에서 더 많이 배운 날

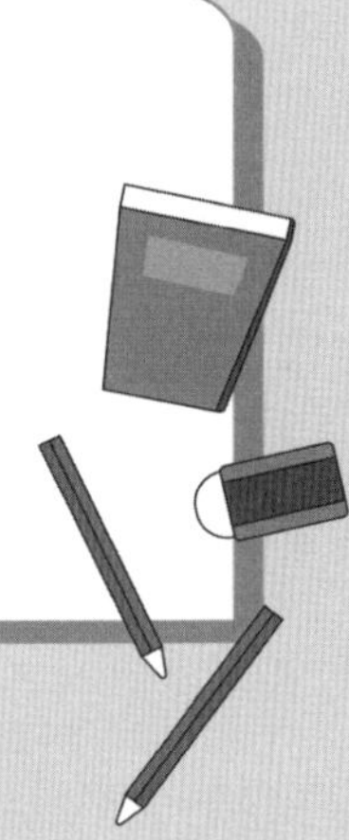

교실 밖에서 더 많이 배운 날

• • • • •

공립학교에선 수업이 거의 다 교실 안에서만 이루어졌지.
정해진 교과서, 칠판, 그리고 받아 적기.
물론 그런 방식에도 나름의 의미가 있었지만,
뭔가 '살아 있는 공부' 같진 않았어.

그런데 국제학교에 와서 체험학습이라는 걸 처음 제대로 겪었을 때,
정말 깜짝 놀랐어.
이건 소풍이나 수학여행 같은 '행사'가 아니라
진짜 '수업'이더라고.

또 다른 수업에선 사회적 기업을 만드는 프로젝트를 했어.
팀을 나눠서 가상의 사회적 문제를 설정하고,
그걸 해결할 수 있는 제품이나 서비스를 직접 기획하는 거였지.
로고도 만들고, 예산도 짜고, 피치 영상까지 찍어서 발표했어.

가끔은 학교 안에서도 체험 수업이 이뤄졌어.
예를 들면 '중세시대' 단원을 할 때,

교실을 실제로 중세시대처럼 꾸며놓고
학생들이 노예, 군인, 왕 역할을 맡아
가상 속에서 선택을 해야 했던 수업도 있었지.
그 상황 안에서 느낀 감정은,
어떤 책 속 문장보다 오래 기억에 남았어.

이런 수업의 공통점은 하나야.
배움이 '진짜 내 일'처럼 느껴진다는 거.
이건 점수를 위한 공부가 아니라,
정말 내가 세상을 이해하고 바꿔가기 위한 공부였어.

그리고 그날 배운 것들은,
시험이 끝나도, 방학이 와도 잊히지 않았어.

The Days I Learned the Most Outside the Classroom

At my public school, almost all learning took place inside the classroom.

Textbooks, blackboards, and lots of note-taking.

Of course, that style of learning had its value,

But it never really felt like living knowledge.

That's why I was so surprised the first time I experienced a proper field study at the international school.

It wasn't just a "school trip" or a "special event" —

It was a real class.

In another class, we worked on a project to create a social enterprise.

In teams, we chose a fictional social issue

and designed a product or service that could solve it.

We created logos, calculated budgets, and even filmed pitch videos to present.

Sometimes, we even had hands-on experiences inside the classroom.

For example, when we were learning about the **Middle Ages,**

our classroom was transformed to look like that time period.

Each student took on a role — a servant, a soldier, or even a king

and we had to make decisions based on different scenarios.
The emotions I felt during those moments stayed with me
much longer than anything I read in a textbook.

All these lessons had one thing in common:
learning felt real.
It wasn't just about getting a grade.
It was about understanding the world — and maybe even
changing it.

And the things I learned on those days?
They didn't fade after the test.
They stayed with me — even through vacations, even now.

발표는 '벌칙'이
아니라 '무기'

발표는 '벌칙'이 아니라 '무기'

공립학교에 다닐 때, 발표는 거의 벌칙처럼 느껴졌어.
손발이 떨리고, 목소리는 작아지고,
앞에 나가는 순간 머릿속이 새하얘졌지.
"틀리면 안 된다."라는 생각이 머릿속을 가득 채우고 있었으니까.

그런데 국제학교에서는
발표가 단순히 '지식을 말로 전달하는 행위'가 아니었어.
내 생각을, 내 방식대로 표현하는 훈련이었지.

처음엔 짧은 의견 나누기부터 시작했어.
"이 문제에 대해 너는 어떻게 생각해?"
"이 장면을 다른 시선으로 해석해 보자."
그런 질문을 수업 중에 **매일** 듣다 보니
자연스럽게 내 목소리를 내는 데 익숙해졌어.

규모가 점점 더 커졌지.
소규모 발표, 그룹 프레젠테이션, 토론 수업,

나중엔 전 학년 앞에서 하는 전교 프레젠테이션까지.

그 과정에서 배운 건 단 하나야.
'잘 말하는 사람'보다 '진짜 자기 생각을 가진 사람'이 더 멋지다는 거.
말을 유창하게 못 해도 괜찮아.
중요한 건 그 안에 담긴 생각이었어.
듣는 사람들도 그런 걸 귀 기울여 줬고.

심지어 어떤 발표에선
슬라이드 없이 그냥 이야기만으로도 큰 박수를 받은 친구도 있었어.
진심이 담긴 이야기엔 언어보다 더 큰 힘이 있다는 걸
그때 느꼈지.

그리고 지금 돌이켜보면
그 발표 하나하나가 나를 만들어 주는 경험이었어.
이젠 사람들 앞에 서는 게 무섭지 않아.
오히려 '내 생각을 나눌 수 있는 기회'로 느껴져.

그 변화의 시작은,
"너의 이야기도 듣고 싶어."라고 말해주는 선생님들과 친구들이 있었
기 때문이야.

<h1 style="text-align:center">Presentations</h1>

: Not a Punishment, But a Superpower

When I was in public school, presentations felt almost like a punishment.

My hands would shake, my voice would shrink,

and my mind would go completely blank the moment I stood in front of the class.

All I could think was, "I can't mess this up."

But at my international school,

Presentations weren't just about delivering information.

They were about expressing your thoughts in your way.

We started small — just sharing quick opinions.

"What do you think about this issue?"

"How would you interpret this scene from a different angle?"

We heard questions like that every single day in class,

and slowly, I got used to speaking up.

Then the presentations grew bigger:

small group shares, group presentations, debate-style discussions,

and eventually, school-wide presentations in front of the whole grade.

But throughout all that, I learned one core lesson:

It's not about being the best speaker,

It's about having something real to say.

Even if your delivery wasn't perfect,

What mattered was the thought behind your words.

And the audience respected that.

I once saw a student give a presentation without any slides —

just speaking from the heart —

And they received the loudest applause.

That's when I realized:

A genuine story can be more powerful than perfect language.

Looking back,

each one of those presentations shaped me.

Now, I'm no longer scared of standing in front of people.

I see it as a chance —

a chance to share my thoughts.

And that transformation began

because I had teachers and classmates who constantly said,

"We want to hear what **you** think."

세상이 교과서가
되는 순간

세상이 교과서가 되는 순간

국제학교에 다니면서 가장 크게 달라진 건,
내가 세상을 보는 방식이었어.

공립학교에 있을 땐, 공부는 교과서 안에 있었고,
세상은 그 교과서 밖에 있는 느낌이었어.
하지만 국제학교에서는,
세상 자체가 교과서가 되는 순간이 많았어.

예를 들어, 어느 날 UOI 시간에
'기후 변화'에 대한 수업을 했었는데,
선생님이 단순히 자료를 보여주시는 게 아니라
"지금 이 문제에 대해 우리가 할 수 있는 일이 뭐가 있을까?"라고 물으
셨어.
그러면서 다 같이 학교 안에서 플라스틱 사용 줄이기 캠페인을 기획하
게 됐지.
이건 그저 과제로 끝나는 게 아니라,
진짜로 학교 전체에 영향을 줄 수 있는 프로젝트였어.

또, 다른 수업에선
한 학생이 난민 문제를 다룬 뉴스 영상을 보고 울었어.
그 친구는 수업 후 직접 자료를 더 찾아보고,
다음 시간에 친구들에게 자기가 조사한 내용을 발표했지.
그걸 보고 나도 충격받았고,
우리가 배우는 게 정말 현실과 연결되어 있구나 싶었어.

공립학교에서는 이런 감정이나 반응을
"감성적이다."라고 치부하고 넘어갔을지도 몰라.
하지만 여기선 그 감정이 바로 배움의 시작이라고 말해줘.
"너의 감정이 왜 그런지를 탐구해 보자."
"너의 생각을 더 깊이 파고들어 보자."
이런 말들이 교실 안에서 흔하게 들려.

그리고, 이건 나 혼자 느낀 게 아니라
내 친구들도 똑같이 느꼈던 거야.

"우리 지금, 그냥 교과서 한 장 넘기는 게 아니라
세상을 한 조각씩 이해하고 있는 것 같아."
어느 날 친구가 이렇게 말했는데,
그 말이 머릿속에 오래 남았어.

국제학교의 수업은 나에게
세상을 바라보는 프레임을 바꿔줬어.

예전엔 '이건 공부랑 상관없는 일'이라고 여겼던 것들이,
지금은 '이건 너무 중요한 이슈고, 내가 생각해봐야 할 문제'로 보이게
됐어.

지금 내가 배우는 건,
시험을 위한 지식이 아니라
세상 속에서 내가 할 수 있는 역할을 찾는 연습이라는 걸
조금씩 깨닫게 된 거지.

When the World Becomes the Textbook

One of the biggest changes I experienced at my international school
was how I began to see the world differently.
Back in public school,
learning felt like it was trapped inside textbooks,
while the real world existed outside of them.
But at my international school,
there were so many moments when the world itself became the textbook.

I remember one UOI class where we were learning about climate change.
Instead of just showing us slides,
the teacher asked,
"What can we actually do about this problem — right here, right now?"
That one question led us to create a school-wide campaign
to reduce plastic use.
It wasn't just a classroom project —
it actually changed something in our community.

In another class,
we watched a news video about the refugee crisis.

One of my classmates was so moved, they started crying.

After class, they kept researching the topic,

and in the next lesson,

they gave a presentation with all the new information they had found.

Watching that, I was shaken too.

I realized that what we were learning wasn't separate from the world —

it was the world.

In a public school,

reactions like that might've been seen as "too emotional."

But here, emotions are seen as the starting point of learning.

Teachers say things like,

"Let's explore why you feel that way,"

And

"Let's dig deeper into your thoughts."

Those kinds of questions are part of everyday conversations in class.

And I know I'm not the only one who feels this way.

One day, a friend of mine said:

"It doesn't feel like we're just flipping pages in a textbook···

it feels like we're actually understanding pieces of the world."

That sentence stuck with me.

Classes at my international school changed the frame I use to see the world.

Things I used to think had nothing to do with school
now feel like the most important issues to think about.

I'm starting to understand:

I'm not just learning information for a test.

I'm learning how to find my place in the world —

and what I can do to make a difference.

교실 밖의 배움
: 수업은 끝나도, 공부는 계속돼

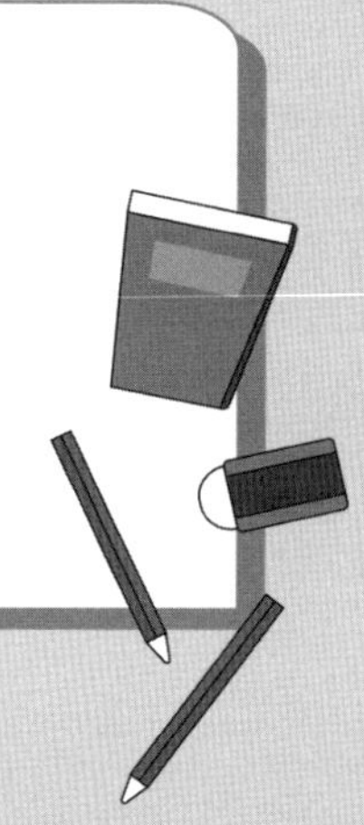

교실 밖의 배움: 수업은 끝나도, 공부는 계속돼

국제학교에서 공부하면서 제일 신기했던 건,
수업이 끝난 뒤에도 배움이 계속된다는 거였어.

공립학교에선 보통 종이 울리면 공부는 끝.
그다음은 학원 숙제나 시험 준비가 기다리고 있었지.
근데 여기서는 수업이 끝난 뒤에도
친구들이 수업 내용을 계속 얘기해.
"아까 그거 진짜 흥미롭지 않았어?"
"나는 좀 다르게 생각했어."
이런 식으로, 수업을 넘어 배움이 이어지는 거야.
누가 시켜서 하는 게 아니라
그냥 궁금하니까, 말하고 싶으니까 이야기하는 거지.

가끔은 쉬는 시간이나 점심시간에도
선생님께 가서 아까 배운 거에 대해 더 물어보기도 해.
선생님들도 항상 "좋은 질문이야."라면서
반갑게 대답해주시고, 오히려 더 많은 질문을 던지시기도 하지.

그럴 때마다 '공부'라는 게 꼭 책상 앞에 앉아 있어야만 되는 게 아니라는 걸 실감했어.

무엇보다도 국제학교에서는
'정답'을 맞히는 능력보다, 스스로 '질문'을 던지는 능력이 더 중요하다는 걸 느꼈어.
그 질문들은 꼭 교과서 안에 있지 않아.
학교 도서관에서 우연히 읽은 기사, 친구랑 하교길에 나눈 대화,
혹은 동아리 활동 중 생긴 고민에서 시작되기도 해.
그렇게 작고 개인적인 호기심이,
하나의 프로젝트로 자라나기도 하고,
선생님과의 멘토링으로 연결되기도 했지.

또, 국제학교는 실패하는 경험조차도 배움으로 여겨줘.
한 번은 동아리 발표 준비를 하다가
정말 시간에 쫓겨 완성도 낮은 결과물을 냈던 적이 있었어.
근데 발표가 끝난 뒤, 선생님은
"이 경험에서 너는 뭘 배웠니?" 하고 물었지.
그 질문이 꽤 충격이었어.
공립학교에선 '망쳤다'고 느낄 상황인데,
여기선 그 자체가 배움의 일부였던 거야.
그때 알았어.
국제학교에선 완벽함보다 과정과 성장이 훨씬 더 중요하다는 걸.

그리고 그런 분위기 덕분에

학생들도 서로 경쟁보다는 협력을 많이 해.

프로젝트를 함께 준비하면서,

어떤 친구는 기획을 잘하고, 어떤 친구는 발표를 잘하고,

또 누군가는 기록을 정리하는 데 강점을 보이거든.

서로의 역할을 인정하면서

"이건 네가 잘하니까 부탁해!"라고 말할 수 있는 문화.

그게 교실 밖 배움의 진짜 힘이 아닐까 싶어.

Learning Beyond the Classroom
: The Bell Doesn't End the Lesson

One of the most surprising things I discovered at an international
school
was that learning doesn't stop when class ends.
Back at my public school, the bell usually meant the end of
studying.
After that, it was all about cram school homework or preparing
for the next test.

But here, even after class,
my friends kept talking about what we'd learned.
"Wasn't that part really interesting?"
"I actually saw it a little differently."
Learning didn't end when the teacher stopped talking —
it continued, not because someone told us to,
but because we were curious,
because we wanted to keep thinking and talking.

Sometimes, during breaks or even at lunch,
we'd go to the teacher to ask more questions.
And they always welcomed it.
"Great question," they'd say with a smile,
and often they'd throw another question right back at us.

That's when I realized:

learning doesn't only happen at a desk.

More than anything, I've learned that

in international schools, it's not about having the right answers.

It's about asking your own questions.

And those questions don't always come from a textbook.

They can start from a random article I read in the library,

a walk home conversation with a friend,

or a problem I noticed during a club activity.

Sometimes a tiny, personal curiosity

grows into a full-blown project,

or turns into a mentoring relationship with a teacher.

And even failure becomes part of the learning.

Once, while preparing for a club presentation,

we rushed everything and ended up with a pretty poor result.

After the presentation, instead of criticizing us,

the teacher simply asked,

"What do you think you learned from this experience?"

That question hit me hard.

In my old school, I would've just thought, "We messed up."

But here, even failure was part of the process.

That's when I realized:

what matters most here isn't perfection —

it's growth.

And maybe because of that atmosphere,

students collaborate more than they compete.

While working on projects, we notice things:

One friend is great at planning,

another is a confident speaker,

and someone else has a knack for organizing the details.

We learn to say,

"You're really good at this — can I count on you for that part?"

That kind of trust and teamwork?

That's the real power of learning beyond the classroom.

방과후는 진짜
내가 나오는 시간

방과후는 진짜 내가 나오는 시간

국제학교에서 가장 좋았던 것 중 하나?
방과후 활동, 그러니까 After-school activity였어.

솔직히 처음엔 좀 놀랐어.
공립학교에선 방과후 하면 보충수업이나 자율학습 같은 걸 떠올렸거든.
근데 여기선 그게 아니야.
진짜 내가 해보고 싶은 걸 해볼 수 있는 시간이었어.

친구들마다 선택하는 게 다 달랐어.
어떤 애는 로봇을 조립하고, 어떤 애는 베이킹을 하고,
또 어떤 애는 축구 연습을 하고 드론을 날리기도 했지.
정말 다양했어.

사실 나는 처음에 After-school 활동 신청서를 받을 때,
고민만 하다가 마감 하루 전에 겨우 낸 사람이야.
뭐가 뭔지도 모르겠고,
'베이킹? 드론? 로봇 만들기?'

이런 게 진짜 수업이 될 수 있다고는 상상도 못했거든.
결국 친구가 하자고 했던 로봇 클럽을 같이 신청했어.
첫날, 책상 위에 복잡하게 생긴 부품들이 잔뜩 놓여 있어서
그냥 "아 망했다…" 싶었지.
근데 선생님이 와서 웃으면서 이랬어.
"처음엔 다 그래. 중요한 건 시작했다는 거야."

그날부터 한 달 넘게,
우린 조를 짜서 움직이는 로봇을 하나 만들었어.
처음엔 바퀴가 제대로 **굴러 가지도** 않았고,
센서를 달았는데 자꾸 벽에 박고,
배터리는 어디에 연결해야 하는지도 몰랐어.

근데 어느 날,
우리가 만든 로봇이
장애물을 돌아서 정확히 골인 지점에 도착했을 때!
진짜 전부가 환호성을 질렀어.
선생님도 우리한테 "이게 바로 도전하고 배운다는 거야."라고 말해줬고.

그때 느꼈어.
"이건 시험지에 답 맞히는 기쁨이랑은 완전히 다르구나."

그날 이후로 나는 방과후 활동을
또 하나의 공부가 아니라

'진짜 나를 알아가는 시간'으로 생각하게 됐어.
어느 날은 친구를 따라 베이킹 클럽에도 가봤는데,
그날은 교실 안에서 밀가루랑 버터 냄새가 솔솔 났어.
우리가 직접 반죽부터 굽기까지 다 했지.
실수해도 다 같이 웃고, 다시 만들고,
그 자체로 너무 재밌었어.
무엇보다 선생님이 "실패도 중요한 경험이야."라고 말해줘서
부담 없이 즐길 수 있었던 것 같아.

스포츠 팀도 정말 인기 많았어.
나는 축구를 했는데,
여기서는 누가 골을 많이 넣었는지보다
어떻게 협력했고, 서로를 어떻게 도왔는지가 더 중요했어.
경기 끝나면 항상 돌아보는 시간이 있었어.
"오늘 우리가 서로에게 어떤 도움이 됐는지"를 이야기하는 시간.
그게 난 참 좋았어.

이런 활동들 덕분에
내가 뭘 좋아하는지,
무엇에 흥미가 있는지
조금씩 찾아갈 수 있었던 것 같아.

여긴 시험 점수도, 등수도 없거든.
잘하든 못하든,

'도전했다는 것 자체'가 인정받는 분위기야.
공부만 하는 학교랑은
정말 완전 다르지?

After School Was When the Real Me Came Out

One of the best things about going to an international school?
Definitely the after-school activities.

To be honest, I was a bit surprised at first.
In my old public school, "after school" usually meant extra study
sessions or self-study time.
But here? It was something completely different.
It was time for me to explore what I truly wanted to try.

Every student chose something different.
Some were building robots, some were baking,
others were practicing soccer or flying drones.
It was all so diverse.

To be honest, when I first got the after-school sign-up sheet,
I stared at it for days and only turned it in the day before the
deadline.
I had no idea what half the activities even meant.
"Baking? Drones? Robot-building?"
I couldn't imagine those could actually count as real "classes."

Eventually, I signed up for the robotics club with a friend who
convinced me.

On the first day, the table was covered with complicated-looking parts,
and I immediately thought, "Oh no⋯ I'm doomed."

But the teacher smiled and said,
"Everyone feels like that in the beginning. What matters is that you started."

From that day on, for over a month,
we worked in teams to build a robot that could move.
At first, the wheels barely turned.
Even when we attached the sensors, the robot kept crashing into walls.
We didn't even know where to plug in the battery.

But then one day—
our robot finally moved around the obstacle course
and reached the finish line perfectly.

We all screamed and cheered!
The teacher said, "This is what it means to challenge yourself and learn something new."

That was the moment I realized:
This joy is completely different from getting the right answer on a

test.

From then on, I didn't see after-school activities as "just another class."

To me, they became a time to really discover who I was.

Trying, Failing, Laughing, Learning

One day I followed a friend to the baking club.

The whole classroom smelled like flour and butter.

We made everything ourselves—from mixing the dough to baking it in the oven.

Even when we messed up, we just laughed and tried again.

It was fun simply because it wasn't about being perfect.

The teacher said something that stuck with me:

"Failure is an important experience too."

That made it easier to enjoy the process without pressure.

Teamwork Over Trophies

The sports teams were also super popular.

I played soccer,

and I noticed that what mattered most wasn't who scored the

most goals—

it was how we worked together and supported each other.

After every game, we'd sit in a circle and reflect:

"How did we help each other today?"

That was my favorite part.

All these activities helped me slowly discover:

What do I really enjoy?

What sparks my curiosity?

There were no test scores, no rankings.

Whether you were good or bad at something,

just trying it was enough to be recognized and encouraged.

Pretty different from a school that's all about studying, right?

쉬는 시간, 그런데
왜 이렇게 자유롭지

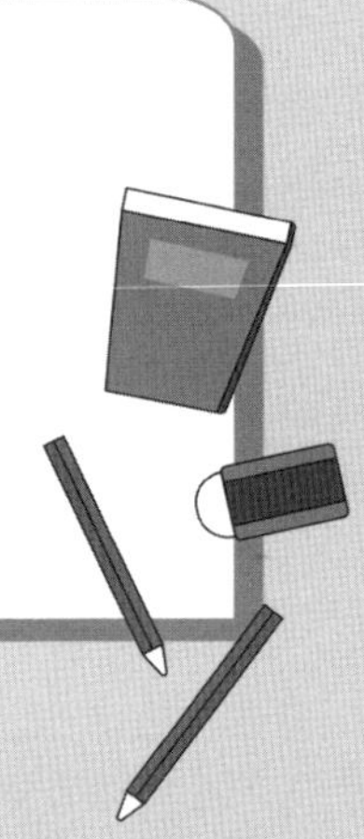

쉬는 시간, 그런데 왜 이렇게 자유롭지?

공립학교에 다닐 때는 쉬는 시간이 딱 10분.
그것도 '쉬는 시간'이라기보다
화장실 갔다 오고, 책 다시 챙기고, 잠깐 물 마시고 나 면 끝났지.

게다가 '자리 이탈 금지' 같은 규칙도 있었고,
복도에서 큰 소리 내면 선생님한테 혼나기 일쑤였어.
쉬는 시간인데도 어딘가 긴장감이 감돌았지.

그런데 국제학교에 오고 나서,
처음 쉬는 시간을 겪었을 때 완전 놀랐어.

애들이 다 복도로 쏟아져 나가더라.
어떤 애는 소파에 누워 있고,
어떤 애는 잔디밭에 나가서 앉아 있고,
심지어 농구공을 들고 운동장으로 뛰쳐나가는 애들도 있었어.

심지어 선생님들도 같이 앉아서 얘기하고 웃고,
어떤 선생님은 아예 학생들이랑 카드 게임을 하고 있었어.

처음엔 속으로,
'이거... 지금 수업시간 맞아?'
'괜찮은 거야? 아무도 안 혼나?'
그랬는데, 이게 여기에선 정상적인 쉬는 시간이었어.

쉬는 시간이라는 게
단순히 다음 수업을 위한 대기 시간이 아니라,
진짜로 머리를 쉬게 하는 시간이라는 걸 느꼈어.

누군가는 음악을 듣고,
누군가는 간단히 간식을 먹고,
어떤 애들은 아예 짧은 산책도 하고 오더라.
그리고 그 덕분에 다음 수업에 들어가면
애들 표정이 확실히 덜 지쳐 보여.

심지어 어떤 날은 쉬는 시간이 길게 잡혀 있어서
선생님이랑 밖에 앉아 얘기하다가
수업 시작 시간이 된 줄도 모른 적도 있어.

가끔은 그 쉬는 시간 덕분에
친구랑 더 가까워지고,

쌤이랑도 수업 밖에서 대화하는 계기가 되기도 했어.

쉬는 시간 하나만 봐도
공립이랑 완전 다른 거야.
국제학교는 마치
"너도 한 사람으로서 존중받아야 해."
라고 말해주는 듯했어.

Break Time? Then Why Does It Feel So Free?

Back at my public school, break time was exactly ten minutes.
But it didn't really feel like a break.
By the time you went to the bathroom, grabbed your next textbook,
and took a quick sip of water, it was already over.

There were rules, too —
"No leaving your seat,"
and "Keep your voice down in the hallway."
Even during breaks, there was this quiet tension in the air.
You couldn't really relax.

But when I came to the international school,
I was shocked the first time break time came around.
Students poured out into the halls —
some flopped onto the couches,
others went outside to sit on the grass,
and a few grabbed a basketball and sprinted to the court.

And the teachers?
Some were sitting and laughing with students,
and one of them was literally playing cards with a group.
I kept thinking to myself,

"Wait⋯ is class over already?"

"Is this⋯ allowed? How come no one's getting in trouble?"

But this — this was a normal break here.

I realized that break time wasn't just

a moment to get ready for the next lesson —

it was a time to truly rest your mind.

Some kids put on music.

Others snacked on something small.

Some even went for a quick walk.

And honestly,

you could see the difference when class started again.

Everyone looked less drained — more ready to learn.

Sometimes, breaks were even long enough

that I ended up deep in conversation with a teacher outside,

not even realizing class was about to begin.

Other times, it was those in-between moments

that helped me grow closer to a friend,

or connect with a teacher beyond the classroom setting.

Even just this one thing —

how break time works —

felt like a completely different world from public school.

At the international school
it's like they're saying,
"You deserve to be treated as a whole person — not just a student."

선생님이랑
농구한다고

"선생님이랑 농구한다고?"

처음 국제학교에 전학 온 지 일주일쯤 됐을 때였어.
그날도 어김없이 쉬는 시간이었고, 나는 그냥 책상에 앉아 있었지.
주변 친구들은 벌써 복도로 우르르 나가고 있었고.

근데 복도에서 들리는 "쿵! 쾅!" 하는 소리.
뭔가 해서 창밖을 보니까
애들 몇 명이 선생님이랑 **농구** 하고 있는 거야.

그것도 그냥 공 몇 번 던지는 수준이 아니라,
2대2 팀 나눠서 진짜 시합처럼 하고 있었어.
웃긴 건, 체육 선생님이 아니었어.
내 Global Perspectives 수업을 가르치는 선생님이었지.

나는 너무 어색해서 그냥 멀뚱히 보고 있었는데,
그 선생님이 갑자기 나를 보더니 손을 흔들면서
"Hey, Siwoo! Wanna join?"
하는 거야.

'내가 지금 뭘 잘못 들은 건가?' 싶었지.
한국 공립학교였으면 선생님이 **농구하기는커녕**,
운동장 나가는 것도 **허락받고** 가야 했잖아?

망설이다가 그냥
"네...?" 하고 나갔는데,
진짜 그냥 아무렇지 않게 받아줬어.
팀도 바꿔가면서, 웃으면서, 진짜 즐겁게 놀았지.

놀고 난 뒤에 선생님이
"이런 게 쉬는 시간이야. 머리를 쉬어야 다시 집중도 잘 되지."
라고 말해줬는데,
그 말이 지금도 기억에 남아.

그날 이후로 나는 쉬는 시간이 기다려졌어.
그 시간 동안 숨을 좀 돌리고,
사람들이랑 얘기하고 웃고 나면,
다음 수업이 그렇게 힘들게 느껴지지 않았거든.

이런 경험이
'학교는 무조건 힘들고 딱딱해야 한다.'라는
내 생각을 조금씩 바꿔 놓았던 것 같아.

"Wait⋯ Is That a Teacher Playing Basketball?"

It was about a week after I had transferred to an international school.

As usual, it was break time, and I was just sitting at my desk while most of my classmates had already rushed out into the hallway.

Then I heard loud thump, thump noises from outside.
Curious, I looked out the window—and I couldn't believe what I saw.

A few students were playing basketball with a teacher.
And not just casually shooting hoops—it was an actual game. Two-on-two. Competitive. Fast-paced.

But the weirdest part?
He wasn't a P.E. teacher.
He was my **Global Perspectives** teacher.

I just stood there, completely confused, until the teacher looked up, saw me watching, and smiled.
He waved and said,
"Hey, Siwoo! Wanna join?"

For a second, I honestly thought I had misheard him.

In my old public school in Korea, not only would a teacher never play basketball with students, we needed permission just to step out onto the field.

But somehow, I found myself saying,
"···Okay?"
And just like that, I was in the game.

No one looked at me funny.
The teacher made room for me, we switched up the teams, laughed, passed the ball around, and just had fun.

Afterward, the teacher said something that stuck with me:
"This is what break time is for. You need to rest your brain so you can focus better later."

From that day on, I actually looked forward to break time.
It wasn't just a pause between classes—it was a chance to breathe, to move, to talk, and to reset.

That one unexpected basketball game started to change the way I thought about school.
Maybe school didn't have to be all stress and structure.
Maybe it could be human.

방학이 '진짜 방학'이 된 순간

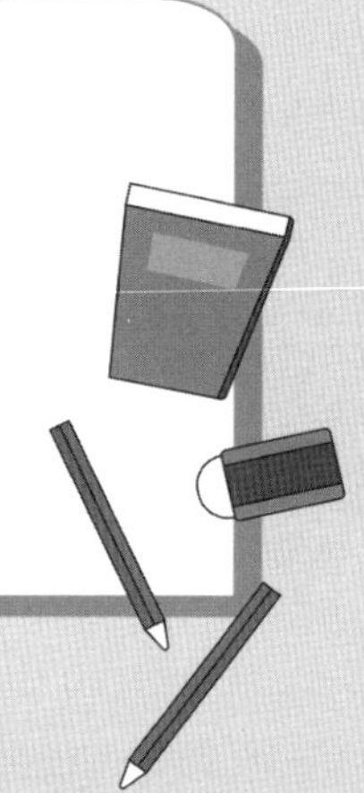

방학이 '진짜 방학'이 된 순간

● ● ● ● ●

국제학교에 다니면서 제일 놀란 것 중 하나.
방학이 진짜 길다는 거야.

한국의 공립학교에 다닐 땐
여름방학이 고작 4주.
겨울방학도 짧았고, 대부분은 보충수업이나 학원으로 채워졌지.

근데 국제학교에 오고 나선
여름방학이 두 달 가까이, 겨울방학도 꽤 길었어.
처음엔 솔직히 걱정했어.
'이렇게 오래 쉬면 수업은 다 끝낼 수 있나?'

근데 조금 지나고 보니까,
그렇게 오래 쉬는 데는 이유가 있더라고.

국제학교의 방학은 단순히 '쉬는 시간'이 아니야.
'내가 뭘 해볼 수 있는 시간'이야.

어떤 친구는 해외여행을 떠나고,
어떤 친구는 그림을 배우거나 캠프에 참가하고,
진짜 다양한 활동을 해.
그리고 그 이야기들이 개학 후에도 계속 이어져.

나도 어느 겨울방학,
그냥 쉬기만 하긴 아깝다는 생각에
근처에서 열리는 농구 캠프에 참가했어.

처음엔 그냥 몸이나 좀 풀자는 마음이었지.
근데 막상 가보니까 분위기가 달랐어.

점수를 내는 게 중요하지 않았고,
코치들은 항상 이렇게 말했어.
"오늘은 뭐가 달라졌는지 생각해보자."
"네가 배운 건 뭐였어?"

매일 훈련이 끝나면
팀원들과 함께 앉아 그날의 경기를 돌아봤어.
어떤 패스가 좋았고, 어떤 장면에서 더 도울 수 있었는지.
누구도 "실수했어!"라고 말하지 않았고,
오히려 실수를 통해 배운 걸 말하는 시간이 있었어.

그 캠프 마지막 날,

코치 한 분이 나한테 물었어.
"Siwoo는 다음에 뭘 더 잘하고 싶어?"
순간 멍했지만,
곧 웃으면서 대답했어.
"팀플레이요. 혼자보다 다 같이 움직이는 게 훨씬 재밌는 것 같아요."

그 질문 하나가 마음에 오래 남았어.
'다음엔 뭘 더 해보고 싶어?'

공립학교에선
방학이 끝나면 늘 아쉬웠어.
"벌써 끝이야?"

근데 국제학교에선
방학이 끝날 때 이런 생각이 들어.
"이제 이걸 바탕으로 또 뭘 해볼 수 있을까?"

농구공을 잡고, 땀을 흘리고, 함께 웃었던 그 방학.
그건 그냥 쉬는 시간이 아니라
나를 조금 더 알아가는 시간이었어.

When Vacation Became a Real Break

One of the things that surprised me most after transferring to an international school

It was how **long** the breaks were.

Back when I was in a Korean public school,

The summer break lasted barely four weeks.

Winter break was also short, and most of that time was spent on extra classes or cram school.

But at the international school,

summer break stretched close to two full months, and winter break wasn't short either.

At first, I honestly worried:

"How do they cover all the material with breaks this long?"

But after some time, I realized—

There's a reason the breaks are so long.

Breaks at an international school aren't just for resting.

They're a chance to ask,

"What do I want to try?"

Some friends travel abroad with their families,

Others take art classes or go to camp.

Everyone does something different—

And those stories continue into the new semester.

One winter break,

I thought it'd be a waste just to relax the whole time.

So I signed up for a nearby **basketball camp.**

At first, I just wanted to move around a bit, get some exercise.

But once I got there, I realized the vibe was completely different.

No one cared about how many points you scored.

Instead, the coaches would always ask,

"What felt different today?"

"What did you learn?"

After every practice,

Our team would sit down and reflect on the game:

What worked well, where we could have supported each other more.

No one said, "You messed up!"—

We talked about our mistakes to learn from them.

On the last day of camp,

One of the coaches asked me,

"Siwoo, what do you want to get better at next time?"

I froze for a second,

But then I smiled and said,

"Teamwork. It's way more fun when we move together than just playing alone."

That question stuck with me:

"What do you want to try next?"

Back in public school,

When vacation ended, I always felt disappointed.

"Is it over already?"

But at an international school,

When the break ends, I find myself thinking,

"Now what more can I do with everything I just experienced?"

That break, running across the court, sweating, laughing with teammates—

It wasn't just time off.

It was a time to get to know myself a little better.

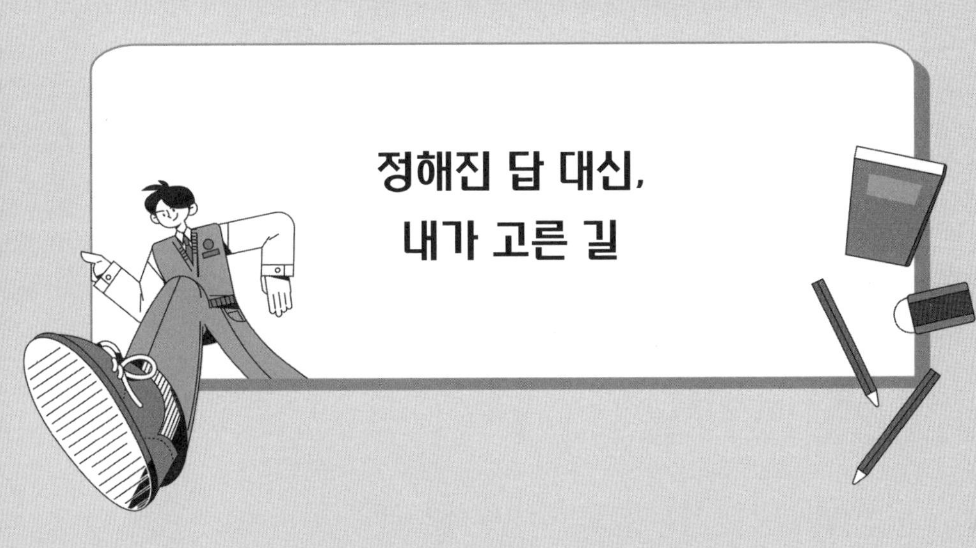

정해진 답 대신,
내가 고른 길

정해진 답 대신, 내가 고른 길

공립학교에선 대부분의 것이 이미 정해져 있었어.
무슨 과목을 듣는지, 어느 페이지를 공부하는지,
시험은 어떤 형식으로 나오는지까지 전부 말이야.
우리는 그 틀 안에서 열심히 외우고, 잘 따라가는 게 '공부'라고 생각했지.
'틀리지 않는 것'이 목표였고, 선생님의 기준에 맞는 답을 찾는 게 전부였
어.

하지만 국제학교에 온 뒤로,
공부에 대한 생각이 완전히 뒤집혔어.

여기선 내가 뭘 선택하는지가 공부의 시작이야.
그게 과목이든, 프로젝트 주제든, 심지어 팀원까지.
"네가 선택한 만큼 책임도 네가 져야 해."라는 식의 분위기였지.
어쩌면 무섭게 들릴 수도 있지만,
그게 오히려 내가 한 사람으로 대우받는 느낌이었어.

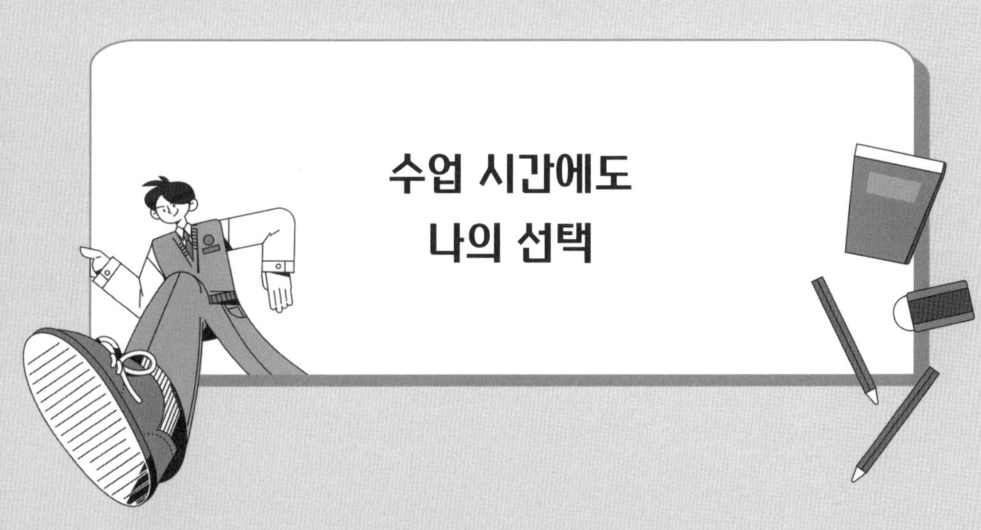
수업 시간에도
나의 선택

수업 시간에도 나의 선택

어떤 날은 선생님이 교과서도 없이 이렇게 말했어.

"오늘은 지난 시간에 다룬 이슈 중
너희가 더 깊이 파보고 싶은 걸 자유롭게 골라봐."

나는 친구 몇 명과 팀을 짜서,
'소셜 미디어가 청소년의 자존감에 미치는 영향'이라는 주제를 선택했어.
그건 나와 내 친구들의 실제 고민이기도 했고,
그래서 더 몰입해서 조사하고, 발표까지 준비했지.

그때 처음 느꼈어.
공부가 누군가의 기준에 맞추는 게 아니라,
내 문제에서 시작할 수도 있다는 것.

"넌 왜 그걸 골랐어?"

또 기억나는 건,

과목 선택 시간표를 받을 때였어.
친구들은 대부분 '인기 과목'을 고를 때,
나는 Media Studies를 택했거든.

그때 선생님이 내게 물었어.

"넌 왜 그걸 골랐어?"

나는 잠깐 멈칫했지만, 곧 대답했어.

"세상을 보는 방식이 영상이나 이미지로 바뀌고 있어서
그걸 좀 더 알고 싶었어요."

선생님은 고개를 끄덕이며 웃었고,
그 순간이 아직도 기억에 남아.
단순한 과목 선택이 아니라,
내가 '무엇에 관심 있는 사람인지'를 표현한 순간이었으니까.

그리고 그 이후로도 계속 이런 질문을 받게 돼.

- **"왜 이 방법을 선택했어?"**
- **"다시 한다면 뭘 바꾸고 싶어?"**
- **"이 과정을 통해 너는 뭘 배웠어?"**

이런 질문들 속에서,

나는 점점 더 '생각하는 법', 그리고 **'나를 설명하는 법'**을 배웠어.

그건 시험문제 100점을 받는 것보다 훨씬 더 어려운 공부였지.

하지만 더 오래 남았고, 더 자주 떠오르는 공부였어.

국제학교는 ‘답’보다
‘과정’을 묻는 곳

국제학교는 '답'보다 '과정'을 묻는 곳

• • • • •

국제학교에서의 공부는,

내가 어떤 과정을 통해 그 생각에 도달했는지를 중요하게 여겨.

정답을 맞췄는지보다,

어떻게 생각하고, 어떤 자료를 찾고,

어떤 기준으로 결론을 내렸는지를 평가하는 거지.

한마디로,

"틀렸어?"보다

"어떻게 여기에 도달했어?"가 더 중요해.

그게 내게 자유를 줬고,

그 자유 속에서 나는 점점 나만의 생각을 가진 사람이 되어갔어.

이게 바로,

정해진 답 대신, 내가 고른 길을 걷는 공부.

그리고 그 길 위에서

나는 단지 '학생'이 아니라,

생각하는 한 사람으로 자라고 있었어.

Choosing My Own Path
Instead of Following the Right Answer

Back in public school, almost everything was already decided for us.

Which subjects to take, which pages to study,

even what the exam questions would look like—

it was all planned out in advance.

We believed that "studying" meant memorizing hard

and following instructions well within that system.

The goal was to avoid mistakes

and find the answer that matched the teacher's expectations.

But once I came to an international school,

my entire idea of learning turned upside down.

Here, learning starts with choice.

Whether it's the subject I study, the topic of a project,

or even the people I work with, it begins with me.

And with that freedom came responsibility—

"If you choose it, you own it."

At first, that sounded kind of scary.

But strangely, it also felt like I was finally being treated as a real

person.

Even in Class, I Had a Say

One day, our teacher walked into class—without a textbook—and said,
"Today, pick an issue from last week's discussion
that you want to explore more deeply."

My group chose the topic:
"How social media affects teenagers' self-esteem."
It was something we all personally related to,
so we were naturally more engaged in researching and presenting it.

That was the first time I realized—
learning doesn't have to start from someone else's standard.
It can begin from our own questions.

"Why Did You Choose That?"

I still remember getting my subject selection form.
While most students chose the popular courses,
I picked **Media Studies.**

My teacher asked,
"Why did you choose that?"

I paused—but then answered,

"Because the way we see the world is changing—

it's becoming more visual.

I want to understand that better."

He nodded and smiled.

It was a small moment, but one I still remember.

Because for the first time,

a subject choice wasn't just about academics—

it was about who I was, and what I cared about.

And ever since then, I've been asked questions like:

- "Why did you choose this method?"
- "What would you do differently next time?"
- "What did you learn from this process?"

Through those questions,

I slowly learned how to **think critically**—

and how to **explain who I am.**

It was a harder kind of learning

than just getting a perfect score.

But it stayed with me longer,

and I found myself thinking about it more often.

A School That Values Process Over Answers

At my international school,

what matters isn't just the final answer—

it's the journey that got you there.

How you thought about the topic,

what research you did,

and what criteria shaped your conclusion—

that's what gets evaluated.

In short,

what matters more than **"Did you get it right?"**

is **"How did you get there?"**

That gave me freedom.

And within that freedom,

I started becoming someone with my own thoughts.

This is what it means to walk a path you chose,

rather than just chasing the "right" answer.

And on that path,

I wasn't just a student anymore.

I was becoming a thinking human being.

국제학교 학생이 말하는 공립학교 vs 국제학교

1판 1쇄 발행 2025년 12월 15일
지은이 박시우

교정 남상묵 **편집** 이승빈 **마케팅·지원** 이창민
펴낸곳 (주)하움출판사 **펴낸이** 문현광

이메일 haum1000@naver.com **홈페이지** haum.kr
블로그 blog.naver.com/haum1000 **인스타** @haum1007

ISBN 979-11-7374-227-9 (43810)

좋은 책을 만들겠습니다.
하움출판사는 독자 여러분의 의견에 항상 귀 기울이고 있습니다.
파본은 구입처에서 교환해 드립니다.